For Martin

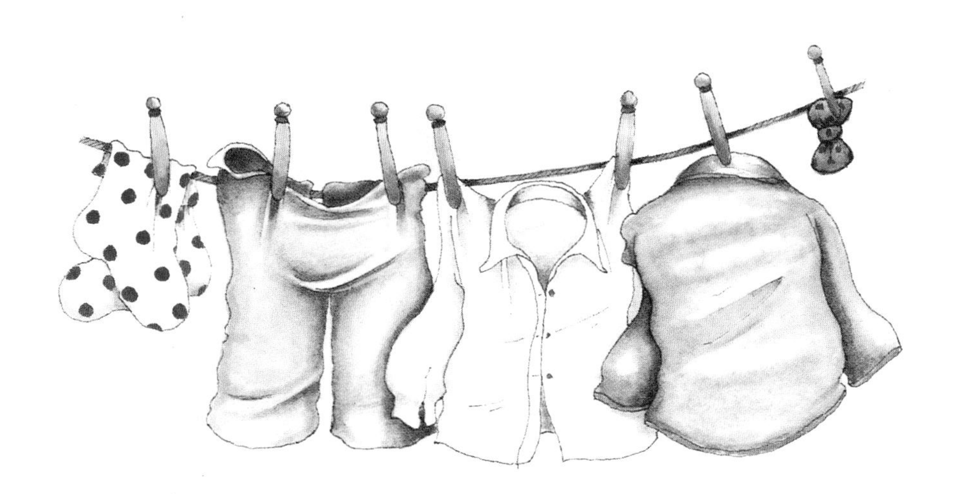

This edition published in 1996 by Leopard Books,
a division of Random House UK Ltd,
20 Vauxhall Bridge Road, London SW1V 2SA

First published in 1993 by Julia MacRae Books

ISBN 0 7529 0166 4

Printed in Singapore

Whoops-a-daisy!

Francesca Simon & Nigel McMullen

LEOPARD

One day Harry's Mummy went shopping,
and Papa came to take care of him.
Papa is Harry's Daddy's Daddy.
Harry was wearing his best jacket,
his best shirt, his best trousers, his best socks,
and his shiny new shoes.
"Harry, how handsome you look," said Papa.

"Now, Papa," said Harry's Mummy,
"Harry's going to a birthday party when
I get back, so don't let him get dirty."
"Don't worry!" said Papa.
After they waved goodbye, Papa and Harry
went outside into the garden.

Harry and Papa played catch, dug a hole to China, and picked two crunchy red apples from the tree. Then Harry helped Papa pull up some weeds.

Heave Ho
Heave *Ho!*
HEAVE HO . . .

WHOOPS-A-DAISY!

Then Harry helped Papa water the roses.

Slip Slop
Slip *Slop!*
SLIP <u>SLOP</u> . . .

WHOOPS-A-DAISY!

Then Harry helped Papa cut some flowers.

Teeter Totter
Teeter *Totter!*
TEETER TOTTER . . .

WHOOPS-A-DAISY!

Then Harry saw the squirrel.

“Squirrel!” said Harry. And he chased him
across the grass, under the hedge
and up the muddy hill.

Glop Slurp
Glop Slurp!
GLOP SLURP . . .

WHOOPS-A-DAISY!

Harry and Papa gathered up Harry's dirty jacket, wet trousers, grimy shirt, soggy socks and muddy shoes, and stuffed everything into the washing machine.

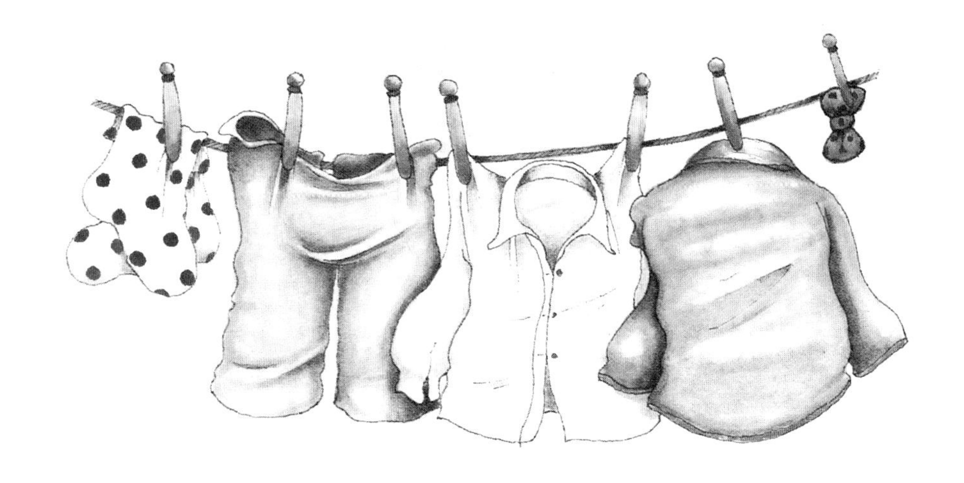

Then Harry and Papa hung all the wet clothes out to dry in the warm sun.
As soon as they were dry, Papa dressed Harry in his crisp clean party clothes.
Harry sparkled like a bright new pin.

When Harry's Mummy came home she was delighted.
"Harry, you smell gorgeous," said Harry's Mummy.
"Just as if you'd been hung out to dry in the sun.
And not a speck of dirt on you.
Papa, how did you do it?"
"That's our secret," said Papa.

Just then the wind blew.
“Oh!” said Harry.
“Don’t worry,” said Papa.

WHOOPS-A-DAISY!